friendly 1

Mr. Know-it-all Crow

By Cindy Leaney

Illustrated by Sue King and Peter Wilks

ROURKE CLASSROOM RESOURCES
The path to student success

Note to Parents and Teachers/Educators
Before reading: Ask your child what this book might be about. Then ask what part of *know* and *crow* sounds the same. Then ask what sound a cat makes (*meow*). Is it the same or different? Remind your child to listen for those sounds in the story.

Written by Cindy Leaney
Designed by Ruth Shane
Illustrated by Sue King & Peter Wilks
Project managed by Gemma Cooper

Created and Designed by SGA and Media Management
18 High Street, Hadleigh, Suffolk, IP7 5AP, U.K.

© 2004 Rourke Classroom Resources
P.O. Box 3328, Vero Beach
Florida, 32964, U.S.A.
Editor: Patty Whitehouse

Printed in China

All rights reserved. No part of this book may be reproduced or utilized in any form or by any means, electronic or mechanical, including photocopying, recording, or by any information storage and retrieval system without permission in writing from the publisher.

ISBN   1-58952-900-6

Mr. Know-it-all Crow

Tell us, please Mr. Know-it-all Crow.

How does rain turn into snow?

5

Why does a cat say *meow*?

And why does a dog bark *bow-wow bow-wow*?

Why does a firefly glow and glow?

Why do flowers grow and grow?

Why does a farmer use a plow?

Why is a sheep a sheep and a cow a cow?

Why does an actor take a bow?

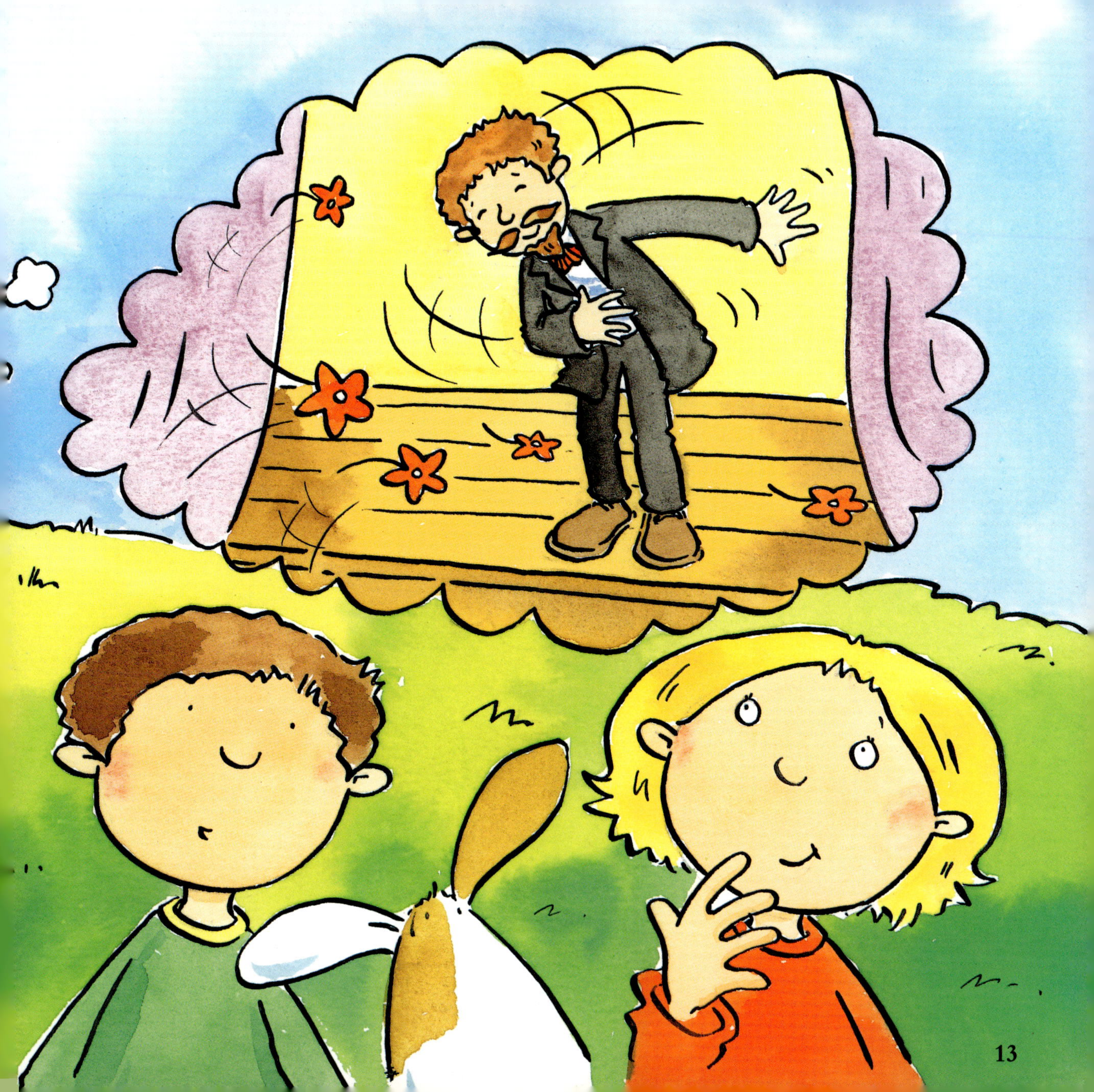

Why is tomorrow such a long time from now?

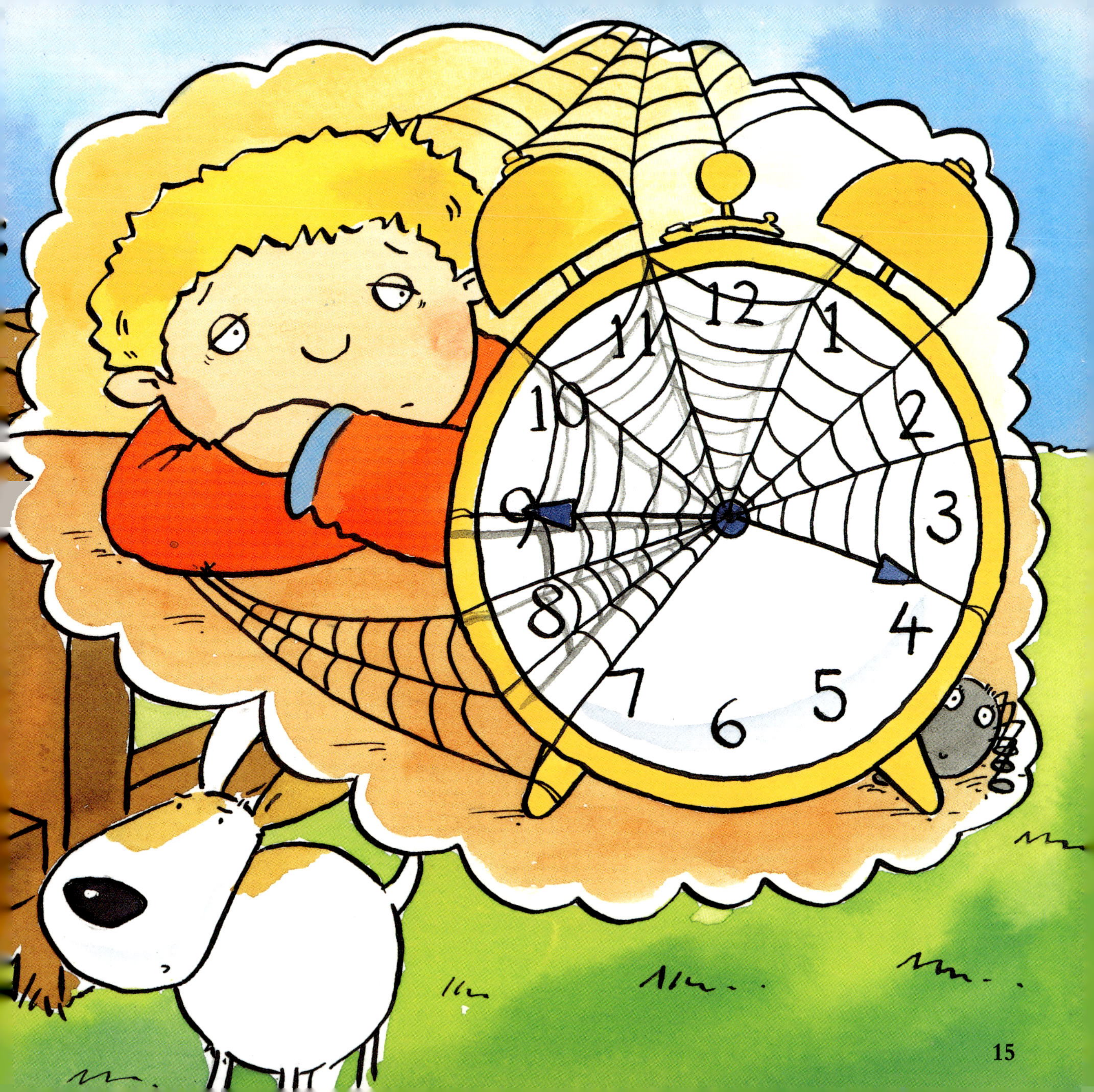
12
1
2
3
4
5
6
7
8
9
10
11

Which is better—fast or slow?

Why do birds sing and rivers flow?

Why do trees have shade and why do I have a shadow?

Why is this flower red and that one yellow?

What is at the end of a rainbow?

Well, how should I know?

So, why do they call you
Mr. Know-it-all Crow?

They don't, you see, my name is Joe!

Game time!

Here are some more *ow* words. Do they rhyme with *crow* or *how*?

a. window b. now c. below d. low e. show f. how g. brown

Answers: crow: a, c, d, e; how: b, f, g.

Look at the pictures. What are the missing letters?

_ow

_ow

Answers: cow, bow.

__ow_

__ow_

Answers: frown, brown.

_____ow

_____ow

Answers: window, yellow.

24